A BIKER MC GOT ME

Butch

JUST BAE

ISBN: 978-1-925988-55-0

CONTENTS

Chapter 1	1
Chapter 2	12
Chapter 3	26
Chapter 4	43
Acknowledgments	61

"You think you might want to do some work?" Ruby, the office manager said, looking over at Kitty, her twenty-year-old stepdaughter who didn't say anything, staring out of the window to the parking lot.

"Get away from that window. Those boys over there got you in trouble in the first place," Ruby said walking through the cluttered motorcycle shop's office and slumping into her chair.

Since her maternity leave ended, Ruby has been on edge with everyone at the bike shop. She was grateful, her husband Mac let her work and didn't leave her home with their infant Jay and daughter, Goldie.

"That stack of invoices over there, Gracie. Please hand them to me," Ruby said. "Those needs to be filed away by the end of the day."

"Okay."

Ruby remembers she's done worse things back when she was younger than her stepdaughter Kitty. She had run away by the time she was twenty. But this time, Kitty was in trouble for hanging out with the bikers and coming home drunk at four in the morning. Ruby found out that Butch was there who pulled Kitty out as a few fights broke out. It wasn't Kitty's first time with Butch at the bar.

"Did you learn your lesson?"

"I did, Mom."

"I don't believe you."

"Well, I don't know if I learned my lesson then."

Ruby got up from her chair and Kitty's eyes widened.

"I'm kidding, Mom. I did—"

"You'd better. What if something would have happened to you? Your father would be devastated if anything bad happened to you."

"I'm sorry." Kitty went back to the filing cabinets.

"Things still rough with her, huh?" She turned back to Gracie, who was the office secretary.

"Yeah but the girl hates me like I'm the one who's wrong. She says I'm being too hard. She's still twenty, not twenty-one."

"I don't think you are. You're concerned, that's all."

"I know but she always such a bitch, I could skin her skinny ass alive." Ruby puts her hand on her head. "But for some reason, Mac loves her to death, he lets her away with murder."

Gracie chuckled. "Besides, how's Mac these days anyway? Haven't seen him around the shop lately?"

"He's okay. He likes spending time at home with the little ones. Hey, speaking of Mac—I'd better go. I'm supposed to cook dinner for his mother tonight. Oh God! Why me?"

"You coming in tomorrow?"

"No, I'm off. Thank God!"

"Well, I'll see you Sunday night for dinner. Remember?"

"Shit, I do. Thanks for reminding me, girl."

Butch stepped away from the bike garage with car oil on his face and uniform. He lit up a cigarette. The sound of a woman's heels hitting the pebbles made him turn; it was Ruby leaving.

They barely spoke these days because of what happened with Kitty at the bar that night and rumors that he was seeing her husband Mac's daughter, Kitty around the town.

Butch's woman, Minnie had skipped town for good, leaving Butch in a drunken wreck. Everyone in town had done their best to try and help him out but the man was stubborn. He'd treated Minnie badly but she treated him worse.

Ruby had tried talking to him about getting back with Minnie but it would always turn into a huge argument. Her husband, Mac told her to stop talking to Minnie before Butch kills himself over her.

"You okay, Ruby?" Butch said for the first time in ages.

"Gotta run home and watch my Jay," Ruby said hurrying. "Butch, wait. Do you got a minute?"

"Yeah, what's up?"

"I want to say sorry for blowing up. Thank you for Kitty, you know."

"No worries."

"Can we forget it ever happened?"

"We can." Butch put his arm around Ruby and hugged her.

"I hate to break up your little reunion," Mac said pulling up on his bike to the entrance of his shop.

"Your hubby's here," Butch said. "Stay gold, lady."

"Thanks, Butch. See ya."

"See ya."

Ruby walked pass by her husband, Mac but slapped him first. "You left my baby alone at home?"

"Hey, I didn't. Goldie's there. A hard-working man don't get a kiss goodbye?" Mac said grabbing Ruby's ass as Butch watched.

Ruby then grabbed Mac by the balls and kissed his cheek. "See you and Mister

Dee later."

Ruby's baby Jay was sleeping, curled up on her chest as she stared at the TV.

"Think I'd better get you to bed, little man," she whispered.

The phone rang and Ruby made it in time after laying Jay down. *It was probably Mac calling to say he'd be home late.*

It wasn't Mac but Minnie, Butch's old lady who skipped town on him.

"Hello!"

"Hey, It's Minnie."

"Oh, hi."

"Just wanted to talk, I missed you guys. You know?"

What the hell? Nobody had heard a word from Minnie in over a month.

"No, I didn't."

"Well, I do."

"Funny way of showing it. What's with you just taking off like that?"

"I'm sorry. I need to talk to a friend. I don't know anyone out here."

Kitty sighs, "Is everything okay?"

"Yeah, I'm in Jefferson City."

"That's not far."

"No, I'm trying to get myself together. What about you? How are things?"

Minnie drank so much that the Sheriff was ready to throw her out of Helena.

"Same as always."

"And Butch?"

"What about him?"

"How's he holding up?"

"You should call him."

"Ruby, I can't—"

"Minnie—look, I'm not saying this to be spiteful, or whatever. You, guys, were headed down the wrong path."

"Tell him I'm sorry, Ruby at least."

"Absolutely not." *Ruby knew better than to get involved again.* "Butch and I have just made up and if he found out that I was talking to you, he'd be upset."

"So what about me?"

"I'm still *really* pissed at you. You just left without telling me anything. We're supposed to be best friends."

"I know! I'm sorry, really I am. But I had to get out of that place? I was using and all."

Ruby wanted to hang up but Minnie kept talking.

"So, you still working at the shop?"

"Yeah, still part-time with the baby and the clan."

"How are the kids?"

"They're doing well, getting big now."

"That's great! So what are you going to do, just work at Mac's for the rest of your life?"

"You mean, am I ever going back to school?" Ruby put her her hand on her face. "I'm thinking about it."

"You should. You're too smart to be stuck there, Ruby. Where do you think—?"

Ruby hears the pipes of Mac's bike outside. "Look, I got to go."

"Can I call you back?"

"Yeah, okay. Bye."

The phone was back on the receiver before Minnie had the chance to respond.

Ruby went to the kitchen, grabbed a beer and a soda from the fridge and ran back into the living room before Mac came in a few seconds later.

"Got you a beer, Papa Bear."

"Thanks, sweetie."

Kitty got up and kissed Mac and then sat back down to look at TV.

"You okay, Ruby?"

"Yeah, why you asking, baby?"

"Just wondering."

"I'm okay, sugar pie."

"I need to know something—" Mac said popping open his can of beer.

"Need to know what, sugar?"

"You ain't pregnant again, are you, Ruby?"

Ruby almost spits out her soda.

"Hell no! Mac. What the hell are you thinking?"

"Well, I'm just asking. People have been saying you've been bitching around the shop since you got back."

"Well, Mr. Mac, can you ask me a better question next time? Come here. I haven't seen you all day."

Mac gets up and sits next to Ruby. She puts her hand on the crotch area of his Wranglers and opens his zipper.

"What do you have for mama here, Papa Bear?"

"Oh, ma'am. Papa has the whole kitchen."

"Hmm...Mama Bear sees—"

CHAPTER TWO

Butch went to the bar when he got off work. He usually lined up the beers ready for his brothers. Each gave him a nod as they took one and found a seat. Some stood gathering around the pool tables.

His long-time buddy, Dustin sat on his usual stool at the end of the bar, watching as Buffalo, the bartender answered the phone.

"For you, Butch," Buffalo said signaling to the phone.

"Butch here?"

"Hello, darling." Kitty, Ruby's daughter was on the other line.

"Sorry, figured it'd be Minnie calling. What's up sweetie pie?"

"I can't hang out tonight, her highness dumped Jay on me again."

"Okay..."

"Well. I guess I'll see you soon."

"Sure will, my lady." Butch smiled and hanged up the phone.

"Got another girl already?" Buffalo asked.

"No, just a customer. Remember, I had my heart stomped on by a certain brunette around here."

"I'm going out with Uncle Butch," Kitty said to her parents the next time she wanted to go out.

"Your little ass is staying home. Watch your sisters with your mother," Mac said while leaving out with his best friend, Hawk.

"Dad—"

"You heard me, little lady."

Kitty slammed the door and Mac and Hawk got on their bikes.

***

"What's that, the third time in a week?" Hawk said as they rode through the streets. "You'd better watch that Butch, Mac." Hawk cracked two beers and handed one to Mac.

"Like a hawk," Mac said.

They arrive at the clubhouse and Butch walks in seeing Mac and Hawk talking.

"You gossip more than old ladies, you know?" Butch said.

"Kitty's upset she can't hang out with her Uncle Butch. Why's that?"

"I don't know. I know you keep

dumping Jay and Goldie on her and the girl's *tired.* "

"That girl doesn't pay no bills in my house and you don't either," Mac said. "Pour me another one, old man. Might be here for a while," Mac told the bartender.

Mac loved his kids, but Kitty was his oldest and most reckless. She'd been testing his patience ever since she became a teen. She's been creeping around with Butch ever since Minnie left.

Kitty started having feelings for Butch who was thirty years older after one night of bike-riding. When Kitty came home with Butch after midnight, her father Mac and stepmother Ruby were huddled on the couch in the dark, watching a horror movie.

Ruby hit pause on the remote control when she heard a bike's pipes roaring outside.

"Mrs. Warren," Butch said coming in.

"Kitty, what the fuck is this?" Mac said getting up.

"Mac, let me explain," Butch said.

"Kitty, why are you two coming inside my home after midnight?"

"Dad—Uncle Butch took me bike-riding."

Mac had known his error when choosing his last old lady, he was hardly home and Kitty was the result.

"I'm going to bed, Mac. I'll let you deal with this. That's your daughter," Ruby said getting up.

"Good night, Mrs. Warren," Butch said.

"Butch, we'll talk about this later—" Mac followed Ruby upstairs and closed their bedroom door.

"Sorry about them."

"No worries. I've known them since we were kids."

"You're that old?"

"Old enough."

The pair chuckled as they went out into the front yard. Kitty stood on the porch steps watching Butch as he adjusted his helmet. "So, Clubhouse, Friday night?"

"I don't get off 'til ten."

"So? The action doesn't start until around eleven."

"I guess I'll come if I stay home."

"What's going on Friday?"

"Mac and Ruby's taking Jay and Goldie to see their grandmother in Helena."

"Call it a date, then."

"I guess you can call it that."

The pair closed the few feet between them and Butch gave her a kiss on her cheek.

"Stay gold," Butch said going back to the bike. He climbed on and started the engine.

"Good night, Uncle Butch." Kitty waved as Butch backed the bike out of the driveway.

The Warren family sat around the breakfast table in the morning. Goldie scooped Jay from his highchair and Kitty eyed her little blonde sister leave.

"You and Butch have fun last night?" Mac said. Kitty nodded before taking a bite from her toast. "What did y'all do?"

"Went bike-riding."

"I know I'm not minding my own business, but is there something going on with you and—?"

"Uncle Butch?"

"Yeah—I like him. Why?"

There was silence as they continued eating breakfast.

"We need to have a talk?" Mac said while he chewed his food.

"About what?"

"That man who's thirty years older than you."

Kitty looked at her father as if he was crazy.

"I know we count on you a lot to take

care of Jay and Goldie, but this is an old man for God's sake."

"Why Dad? I'm grown. I choose whoever I want to be with." Kitty poured herself another cup of coffee.

"You're not grown in this house, young lady. Do you even pay a bill around here?" Ruby said.

"Yes, I pay—"

"Pay with what? Your looks?"

"I watch my sisters when you guys go out. Is that not paying? Do you know how Goldie feels?"

"Young lady, you're—" Butch said.

"It's not even once in a while." Kitty continued. "It's all the time. I have to cancel my plans all the time..."

"Look, I know sweetheart, but sometimes things just come up. I appreciate you watching your sisters. Don't think I don't?"

Ruby let out a sigh, Mac was always defending her.

"Yeah- my plans. Does she think that

just because I'm working all the time that I don't have a life?" Ruby said.

Mac was now caught in a crossfire.

"Ladies, ladies..." Butch said banging on the table. "Can we eat in peace?"

"Look, Kitty. Butch and I were supposed to go out for dinner last weekend, but couldn't because Jay was sick. Daddy and Mommy need some time, too."

"I'm sorry about that. But I'm your daughter, not Jay and Goldie's nanny."

"We know that."

"Daddy, I want my own life. So, if things don't change... I'll start looking for a place of my own." Kitty made the threat often knowing her father would listen to her eventually.

"Don't you think that's a little drastic? Besides, aren't you going to college in... six months, you can't hold out a little bit longer?"

"College isn't a definite—they might not want me."

"Who are you kidding? Why wouldn't they want somebody as smart as you?"

"We're getting off point here, Mac and Kitty. Now about Butch?" Ruby said.

"What about him? I like him, Ruby."

"Me and your father need to talk about this. Please don't do anything stupid."

"You're right. I need to go get ready to open the office," Kitty said getting up from the table.

"We're not done yet, young lady."

"I don't care..."

It was Friday and Kitty went to the party at the clubhouse and Butch didn't show up. With nobody sober enough to ride her home, she walked to a friend's house from high school. With Mac and Ruby away for the weekend along with her siblings, Kitty finally felt free.

In the morning, Kitty ran into Penn

Bolling, the heiress of Bolling Pharmacy while passing. Penn had been named after her place of conception and hated that name. Her classmates teased her calling Boiling Pen.

"Hey, bitch. How's it going?" Penn said when Kitty came in.

"Could you be quieter? It's too early in the morning for your shit."

"Hey, I heard you're hooking up with Butch Bradford?"

"Who the fuck told you that?"

"Don't worry, I have my sources. Hey you know, I wouldn't blame you at all. It's about time that old man found someone who's his match."

"Don't be a dick, it's not like that."

Butch Bradford was greyed, muscular and so hot. Kitty was always slightly jealous of his old lady, Minnie when she saw them together. As far as Kitty was concerned, it should have been her that got a shot with

Bradford even if she was fifteen. But that brunette vixen had jumped right on in there and stolen his heart. Kitty's crush on Butch had almost vanished by the time Minnie and Butch had fallen out. All she wanted now was finally to get a piece of the blond Adonis.

"Anyways, I just wanted to see if you had plans tonight?" Kitty said after day-dreaming.

"Yeah, Brad Pitt is flying in especially to take me to the diner," Penn said chuckling.

"Well us single ladies should stick to-gether. My folks are away, so if you want to come over—"

"Yes!" Penn put her arm on her friend's shoulder. "I cannot be stuck at home with my parents another night. I'll kill myself—I swear to God."

"Well come over whenever."

"Hey, you want me to bring some peyote over again?"

"Hell no, that shit made me puke up a storm."

"Let me help you out then! I have a special mix that'll get rid of all the toxins you drank last night. It cleanses the spirit, my dear."

"Okay..." There was no arguing with Penn, she would keep talking for days.

Kitty strolled through the aisle as she listened to Penn babble on about...something. She stopped dead in her tracks.

"What the—Texas Garby is in town!"

"That hunk makes me wet every time I think of him. I wish he'd fuck the shit out of me."

Texas Garby was six feet four inches tall of pure-muscle. He had brown-cropped hair and tattoos on his arms and neck.

"I mean?" Kitty whispered. "He's here, girl."

"What? Oh my God! How do I look?" Penn took a few paces back in hopes of not being spotted, but it was too late. Texas was already heading in their direction.

"He's coming. I'll see you later."

Without giving Penn a chance to answer, Kitty started leaving.

"Girl, don't—come back here—"

"Hi, Texas," Penn said.

"Howdy."

CHAPTER THREE

The start of the week began awkwardly when Kitty called from Helena telling her father that she wouldn't be home for Thanksgiving. She had decided to outstay her welcome at her Aunt Ann's house, much to Mac's protests. Mac had wondered if Kitty would ever come back.

Despite the break, Kitty's Thanksgiving had been the worst Turkey Day, ever. Kitty's aunt, Ann had volunteered for a local church's dinner and brought Kitty along. It turned out to be long lines serving the homeless and they barely had a chance to sit down.

Kitty had quickly changed, re-applied her makeup and went out to wait for Butch. He texted her earlier saying he would pick her up from the church for Thanksgiving.

"Hey Kitty," Tiny said. *He was in love with Kitty since grade school and Kitty went out with him once in 9th grade.* Kitty lit up a cigarette and waited for Butch in the church's lot. "Happy Thanksgiving."

"Back at you." She smiled wishing her ride would hurry up. "You meeting your parents here for dinner?"

"No. I came to see if you wanted to come to celebrate Thanksgiving with me." He came closer.

"I have plans already. Just waiting for

my ride, shouldn't be long," Kitty said, moving back.

Tiny put his arm around her and said, "Forget that, I've missed you honey-pie. Let's grab a couple of beers and celebrate together-just you and me."

Kitty knew Tiny was drunk. She remembered the time that she gave Tiny a chance for half a day and then dumped him later that evening.

"Yeah, I can't. As I said, I have plans with my family." Kitty wriggled from him and walked out of the lot into the street.

"What, I'm not good enough now?"

"What?" I told you I'm busy.

Kitty heard the pipes of Butch's bike before she saw him appear from around the corner. She sighed and Butch ignored Tiny as he pulled up beside Kitty.

"Jump on, little sweetheart."

"Oh, I see. You're fucking that old douche bag."

"What the fuck did you say, boy?" Butch said.

"Nothing, don't worry about him. He's drunk." Kitty said grabbing the helmet Butch handed her, trying her best to fasten the straps quickly.

"Hey bitch, I'm talking to you."

"What did you just call her?" Butch said.

"You deaf, asshole?" Tiny's hand just missed Kitty's mouth.

Butch got off his bike but Kitty stood in front of him.

"Butch, please. Let's just go. *Please.*"

"I knew you'd end up some biker trash. That's why your stupid ass ain't shit."

Butch couldn't take it any longer. He set down the kickstand and Tiny ran. Kitty chased after Butch, trying to get in between the pair.

"Butch, just ignore him. Come on, we need to go." She grabbed Butch's hand and attempted to pull him back.

"Muthafucker!"

"You should listen to her? I know the rest of your buddies are waiting to take a turn on her tonight."

Butch freed his arm from Kitty's grasp and punched Tiny in the face, his nose started bleeding and his right eye was swollen.

"Don't you ever talk to my woman like that again, you fucking faggot," Butch said.

"You'll be sorry you did that." Tiny wiped the blood from his face. He was too drunk to fight Butch who just made him a bloody pulp. But he tried, charging at Butch and tackling him to the ground. The pair scuffled and scrabbled, each getting the chance to pound each other's face in.

Tiny had somehow managed to get on top of Butch. His arm raised and his fist kept landing on Butch's face.

The helmet. Use the helmet. Kitty had it in her hand the entire time, holding it by the rim. She dashed over and swung it into

Tiny's face with all the strength she had. He fell back, clutching his jaw.

"Butch, come on and get up. We need to get going...now." Butch was startled and Tiny held her hand out to pull him up.

Since they've known each other, they had never seen each other hit anyone.

"Butch, now."

It was too late; a police cruiser was now at the scene.

Some Dudley Do-Good had called the cops and the three of them ended up in the cells at the sheriff's station. They spent two hours of back and forth questions with Sheriff Roberts and his deputy, Clyde. Finally, Kitty was given a phone call and called her father, Mac. Mac had words with the Sheriff—what those words were, Kitty would never know. But they had worked, eventually, all charges were dropped and everyone walked away as happy campers.

Kitty and Butch finally had got to their Thanksgiving dinner at Firth's Diner. They were pretty quiet during it and once they finished, Kitty went out back to smoke.

"Want some company?" Butch said leaning against the doorjamb watching her.

"Sure."

"You okay?"

"God, I'm just so embarrassed. I'm really sorry that you had to go through that."

"Calm down." He said, nudging her. "There's nothing to be embarrassed about."

"You're kidding, right? Did you miss the part where I had smacked my ex in the face with a helmet?"

Butch laughed, rubbing his face.

"Thanks for that, by the way." He took a pull from his cigarette, trying to stop himself from smiling. "That was kind of hot, you know? Helping an old man out."

"What?"

"You getting all fired up like that."

Before Kitty could say another word, Mac said, "Time to go home, kid."

"Okay, but do we have to?"

"Unless you want to rescue me from fighting your father, I think so."

"I think you're right."

Kitty returned home and things got a lot worse. She cursed out Mac and Ruby one night after coming home late again and got thrown out. She wound up going to Butch's.

Butch's laid-back attitude about everything annoyed her. They had their first argument at dinner, so Kitty took hers to her room. Inside, she could hear her neighbors screaming and all she wanted to do was join in. They were cussing and throwing things around. She also heard them making accusations of who was the worst parent.

"You left my baby with that tramp," the woman said. "You're never even here! Doing god knows what at that clubhouse. If you aren't at that damn place, then you're probably fucking that little huzzie!"

"Shut the fuck up!" The man said and then threw something.

"I fucking hate you..."

Kitty's pillow was doing a poor job of shielding the commotion. She sat up on the bed. *That was it, she was out of there.* She put her shoes on, grabbed her cigarettes, purse, and phone from the dresser table and threw on her leather jacket.

"Where are you going?"

"Out."

"Where?"

"I don't know, okay. Give me your keys." She stopped at the door."I'm sorry. I can't sit up there and listen to this anymore. I need to get out of here. I'll be back."

Kitty climbed onto Butch's black Harley and put the keys into the ignition; once they were in, she let her hand drop into her lap. She had no idea where to go and wound up going back to her parents' home.

"Dad, I'm coming home."

"Why?"

"I just can't take being alone, that's all."

"No more funny stuff. Ruby's not taking your shit neither am I."

"Ok, Daddy."

The peace only lasted twenty-four hours and Kitty was gone again but this time with her bag.

There was only one person left to call again; Butch.

Kitty fished her phone from her pocket, pulled up his contact and stared. She chewed on her bottom lip debating on hitting the call button.

"Screw it. What's worse?" Kitty muttered as she hit the call button. It only took three rings for him to pick up.

"Hey sweetheart, what's up?"

"I'm sorry about the other night. Can I come over? I know it's pretty short notice but..."

"Always got room for you, something wrong?"

"Same shit, different day."

"What?"

"Never mind. You think we can get wasted? Kind of need it."

"Sure. Meet me at my place."

"On my way."

"No problem, see you in a few."

Butch had a bottle of Jack and a set of glasses waiting when Kitty arrived.

He filled them and lit up a joint. Kitty remained quiet, staring at a spot on the dirty carpet. Bitch continued looking at Kitty, noting how those once chubby cheeks seemed to have thinned out some, almost making her look older.

"So, talk to me. What's going on?"

Kitty sat up and took the glass.

"Needed to get out of the house again. It's a nightmare over there."

"Mac's that bad?"

"We fight every night."

"Did you start with them again?"

"No, not this time. I came in late after work and they threw me out again."

Butch handed over the joint. "You think Ruby wants out?"

Kitty nodded as she exhaled a stream of smoke, watching it swirl away before turning her attention back to Butch. "I know she does, Butch. As much as we don't get along, I respect her for sticking around."

"Can I tell you something?" Kitty said suddenly.

"Anything."

"I always wanted to suck your cock, Uncle Butch." Kitty took a few more pulls of the joint before handing it back and taking a sip from the glass.

"What? Girl, what are you saying?"

"Seeing you in that black leather jacket just turns me on."

"I can't. Your father will kill me."

"Why are you worried about him? You can't keep a secret." Kitty put her hand on his crotch and Butch raised his eyebrows.

"I—I can't," Butch mumbled as Kitty pulled his zipper down.

"What are you doing, sweetheart? This is not right."

"It is, Uncle Butch."

Kitty put her hand inside and yanked

his cock out. Butch's red pubic hair gave Kitty thoughts about strawberries.

"Kitty, please—"

"I need something to make me feel better. It's too much shit happening right now. May I?" Kitty goes down and kisses his glans.

"Oh my—"

Kitty jerks Butch's cock and licks him in the ear.

"You'll remember this, Uncle Butch. I'm leaving town for a bit. Don't worry, I'm not leaving you—"

"What? What do you mean?"

"Lay back and let me have fun before I go."

As predicted, Ruby had walked out on Mac two weeks before Christmas. She was done arguing with Mac about Kitty and not being home enough with their kids. Mac had taken that hard and returned to spending most of his time at the clubhouse getting drunk.

Kitty tried to ignore the pain by keeping busy, taking extra shifts at a diner in Clancy. She hated how quiet the place was home but she needed the extra money.

Mac had been less than thrilled that Kitty hadn't informed him of her plans straight away, but he had been happy for her.

He invited her to Sunday dinner and Kitty gladly accepted.

Mac watched his daughter as they sat at the dinner table. Dinner had been over for a while but neither of them had bothered to move.

"You okay sweetheart?"

"Oh yeah. Just thinking about my mom."

"What about her?"

"I don't know." Kitty shrugged. "How much I miss her at the table with us. She passed away too soon."

"I miss her too." Mac nodded. "Come here."

"What for?"

"Because your old man wants a hug. Now, get over here."

"Dad! You're going to squish me to death!"

"You? You're a bag of bones, honey."

Kitty stopped laughing and came to her father.

"Listen to me. I'm really proud of you. Betty (Kitty's mother), would be so proud of you, too. She always knew you'd do well. Now, here comes the real question: How's Butch?"

"He's fine."

"Are you still seeing him?"

"Yeah, he comes around to keep me company, every now and then," Kitty's arms were wrapped tightly around Mac's neck.

"Butch's a good guy. I was upset because you're so young. You need to live your life."

"You're going to make me cry, Daddy." Kitty feels her eyes watering. "I know Dad. It's weird but so is life."

"Love you, sweet-pie."

"Love you too, Daddy."

"Now, get off my lap. You're getting heavy."

Kitty gets up and gathers her things. "Dad, I'll see you for Christmas."

"Ok, sweet-pea. Come early."

"Why?"

"Because you are cooking for your old-man."

CHAPTER FOUR

The days leading up to Christmas had been hectic and Mac's Motorcycle Shop closed at noon on December 24th. The local clubhouse invited all the bikers and their families to prep it for the annual Christmas party.

Kitty and her friends Penn, April Kelly, and Violet were in charge of managing the food and liquor and making sure the Christmas lights and decorations were up.

"Why does this always feel like punishment?" Violet said to Kitty as they made their way over to the boxes of Christmas decorations.

"Could be worse. We could be on clean-up detail, cleaning up trash... with the trash."

"Yeah, that sucks."

"Oh shit! Ruby's here with your sibling," April Kelly whispered.

Kitty looked but didn't move as Ruby walked over.

"Hey, Kitty! You're looking well. How're things going at home with your father?"

"I don't know. I live in Clancy."

"Wha—you moved out?"

"Yeah, Butch and I got a place."

"Hey, at least you have someone to be alone with. You're doing better than I am."

As they were talking, Butch's old girl Minnie came in.

"There goes that tramp!" Minnie ran up to Kitty.

"Hold-hold it now! You're not going to be calling nobody any tramps in here, Minnie. God strike you down," Ruby said with her arms folded. "Especially to my little girl."

"I don't give a fuck who she is. She stole my man."

"Minnie, calm down. Kitty didn't steal nobody. Go sit your ass down over there and pour us a drink. I'll be over in a minute."

Minnie walked away already drunk and said, "You little tramp!"

"Fuck you, bitch!" Kitty said.

"Hey-hey!"

Kitty's friends were giggling and Kitty put up her middle finger.

"Anyway before we were interrupted—"

"How's it going with Mac?" Ruby said.

"Call him and find out."

"Girl, he hates me for taking your sisters."

"I don't know, put the moves on him again. He always said you were his sweet-pea."

"Maybe, I will." Ruby starts walking over to Minnie. "I'll talk to you later, Kitty."

"Ok."

"Good seeing you. I'm so proud of you."

"Thanks."

Minutes later, Butch walks in, with that black leather jacket, with mousse in his hair. He's rugged, unshaven but hot as hell.

"Oh my God! Isn't that Minnie's old man?" Violet said.

"Fuck no! Did you just hear that bitch over there talk shit about me with him?" Kitty said.

"Oh my—you're fucking old Butch."

"Girl, if you don't stop it. We're just friends."

"Well, you won't know if you are more than that until you try." Violet stares."Look at his—"

"Okay, enough of that. We got things to do around here."

***

Butch walks up to Ruby and embraces her while Minnie's looking on drunk as hell. When Butch says hello to Minnie, she responds harshly.

"Hey, Butch. Why are you fucking that handmaiden over there?"

"That's it—" Kitty heard her and ran over. She grabbed Minnie by her hair and dragged her out of the seat. Then, she punched her in the face. Ruby and Kitty's friends broke it up.

"How you like that for a handmaiden, Bitch?"

"I'm going to fucking kill your skinny ass."

"Then do it, tramp."

Kitty grabbed Butch's cock in front of everyone and kisses him for a long time.

"Oh my God! Look at Ms. Skinny," Penn said as April Kelly and Violet put their hands over their mouths.

Minnie was still on the ground and Ruby was holding her back.

"Girl, you are so wrong," Ruby said picking up Minnie to take her outside.

"You see—that whore," Minnie said stumbling.

"Hey, that's the last time. Come on." Ruby said.

"I swear you two are made for each other," Violet said when Butch left to see some of his friends.

"He asked me what I thought about us just yesterday."

"That's great! You said yes, right?" Violet said.

"Hey ladies, want to cut the chat and actually do some decorating?" Kitty's back straightened as she heard the call of the queen; her stepmother. She continued trying to get the damn piece of tinsel to stick to the wall. "Don't make me separate you," Ruby said, narrowing at the girls.

"Sorry, Ruby!" Violet said.

Ruby nodded and headed back to the kitchen.

"You don't think she was standing here the whole time, do you?"

"Girl, you need glasses."

The girls giggled.

Once the decorations were up and Ruby had voiced her approval, it left the girls some time to get ready for the party. They decided to drive to Kitty's place in Clancy for a few hours.

Violet, April Kelly, and Penn had finished way before Kitty and made themselves comfortable on the futon, flipping through magazines.

"Are you done in there?" Violet hollered.

"Almost, give me two seconds."

"Okay, be honest. How do I look?"

"Holy mother!" Penn said tossing the magazine down.

"It's too much, isn't it? I knew it." Kitty bit her bottom lip. She didn't want to look like any of the hookers that would be hanging around the clubhouse. "I need to tone it down some, don't I?"

"No not at all, it's perfect," April Kelly said appraised her from head to foot. The loose messy curls, smoky eyes and bright red lips made her look way older. Kitty's black strapless dress clung to her, accentuating her comely figure and the stiletto Mary Janes made her legs appear curvier and longer.

"Promise that I don't look like a slut?"

"Cross my heart. You look fantastic." The girls made an imaginary cross over their hearts. "Now can we go?"

"Let's go, girls."

***

The bartender, Buffalo had been manning the bar at the Christmas party when Kitty's friend, Violet came over. They had long since vanished together and Buffalo got Mole to take over, promising to make it worth his while. Mole was a tall, skinny kid who was now reaching the end of adolescence.

Kitty was mingling, she thought, going back and forth to grab drinks but drinking them herself.

"What are you drinking?" Mole asked.

"Jack and Coke, please. Could you make it a large one? Oh and a shot of tequila, please."

"For you? Sure."

They smiled and he got to pouring her drink. "You look really good tonight."

"Thanks."

"I'm getting patched soon, you know?"

Kitty ran her hand through her hair. "I heard, congratulations."

"I'd better go say hi to everyone. Catch you later."

"Bye!"

Butch was at the pool table when he saw Kitty at the bar. His concentration had wavered from the men around him as he looked on. He saw Mole was trying to flirt with his lady. He wasn't that surprised, he'd do the same if it were him.

Then she turned away from the bar

and he saw her face- he was floored. That could not be her, *no way*.

Kitty hadn't noticed him staring at her like some slack-jawed idiot.

After finishing up the pool game, Butch went to the bar, making idle chat with Hawk, the second bartender, while he waited for Mole to return from the back with a crate of beer. He looked around the room again, seeing she and Penn were laughing at something April Kelly had said. Once the laughter had subsided, Kitty turned her head in Butch's direction. She kept staring and he fingered for her to come.

Kitty excused herself and walked over to the bar. Butch's eyes didn't move away from her. "Hey, you." She nudged him.

"Hey, little sweet-pea. Having a good time?"

She nodded.

"You look amazing. I think you need

another one." Butch pointed to the empty glass in her hand.

"Think I do." Mole was back standing in front of them waiting, clearing his throat.

"Want to split a bottle of Jack with me?"

"Sure."

"You heard the lady, Mole," Butch said seeing Mole was still checking Kitty out.

"I got to go use the bathroom. Hold that drink. I'll be back." Kitty turned to head but was stopped when Butch grabbed her arm.

"Go use the one in the office, you don't want to see the one in here."

When Kitty had finished checking her appearance, Butch was already on one of the benches, joint in one hand and the opened bottle of Jack in the other. She climbed on the table beside him.

"Hey! You started without me."

Butch handed over the joint, scooting towards her some.

"Sorry, sweetheart." Kitty's head was now resting on Butch's shoulder, looking like she was feeling it from all the Jack. He pulled her closer into his side.

They sat there for a while, only speaking when they passed the bottle. Kitty shifted and began looking around in her purse. She pulled out a small gift box and handed it over to Butch. "I forgot - I got you an early Christmas present."

"What's this?"

"Just wanted to say thanks for taking care of me."

"You didn't have to do that."

"I know, but I wanted to."

"Can I open it?"

Kitty nodded, watching him look at the small box. He tore at the gift wrap until it lay in a heap on the table. Lifting the lid, he peered inside and picked out a silver lighter in his palm, etched onto the surface was an image of the reaper. Butch stayed silent as he ran his thumb over the pattern.

"You like it, baby?"

"I *love* it. Thank you, sweetheart."

Butch wanted to thank her properly, but with the amount of prying eyes around the parking lot, instead, he hugged her. "Your gift is inside if you want it now."

"Sure, why not?"

Butch had walked slightly behind her, the entire way through the clubhouse. They went into the office and Butch was rifling through the dresser drawer as Kitty stood awkwardly, leaning against the desk.

"They're not wrapped, sorry about that."

"I don't mind." She waved before accepting the two boxes. "Two gifts. Well, don't I feel special?" She opened the boxes; a pair of black leather boots, and skull suede hair ties. "They're great, Butch."

"You don't like them?"

"Cross my heart, I do." Kitty put the boxes on top of the desk, wrapped her arms around Butch's neck.

Butch kissed her and Kitty's hands made their way down his chest at the hem of his leather jacket. She pulled to tug his shirt up. "Kitty—"

"This is the present I've been wanting to give you since I've known you."

Butch yanked his shirt over his head, tossed it to the floor and backed Kitty up against the desk.

"Fuck me, Butch. Right here."

Kitty's legs felt as if they might give out when Butch's rough hand slid beneath her. He teased her sensitive bundle of nerves that had her close to hyperventilating.

"Take that dress off, sweety," Butch said.

Kitty complied, unzipping. Butch pulled her from the edge of the desk so he could pull it down with her. His hands tangled in her black thong, working it down her legs. His gaze wandered over Kitty's slim physique.

Meanwhile, Kitty unbuttoned Butch's jeans and with one sharp tug had pulled them down with his boxers. He kicked them out of way, grabbed Kitty by her hips and backed her more on the table. His cock was like a sword ready to strike.

"Are you going to be okay?"

"Yes. Don't hurt me, please with that thing."

She nodded her head, bracing herself on Butch's shoulders as he lowered her hips, enabling him to enter.

Kitty gasped as Butch slid inside. They were still for a moment giving her a chance to fit in with him. Butch's hands were on her hips when Kitty began slowly finding a satisfying rhythm. Her back was arched forcing her breasts towards him, and his hands held on them. Her hands gripped his muscular thighs, not caring if her manicured nails bit into his skin.

"Oh, Fuck—Butch! You are so big! God, I can't take it…"

The rhythm and force increased so quickly that Kitty almost passed out.

"Butch!" She gasped. He grabbed the back of her thigh, forcing her to move her leg. He pushed deeper inside, feeling himself getting closer and closer to cumming, letting out a grunt with each thrust. Kitty was so close and it was almost painful.

A couple more thrusts and the pair were breathless, sweaty yelling each other names.

Then, someone knocked.

"Oh shit!"

"Is someone inside? I need to pee."

"Yeah, it's me, Butch. Who's that?"

"It's Minnie. I need to use the bathroom." She opened the door seeing Kitty and Butch on the table naked.

"Oh my God! You fucking bitch!"

"Hold it, hold it—Minnie," Butch said. "Close the door and come inside."

"I'm going to kill you and that bitch."

"No, you're not. Just come in."

"Kitty started putting on her bra and Butch whispered something to her.

Minnie came in and closed the door.

"What do you want, Butch?"

"Take off your clothes."

"What the fuck, Butch?" Kitty and Minnie said at the same time.

"You heard me. We're going to settle this one and for all. Now, do as I say."

ACKNOWLEDGMENTS

Thanks for reading and please leave a review. This will really help us out.

Consider joining our mailing list by sending us a hi at therealjustbae@gmail.com. We give out FREE Audiobook codes all the time.

Join our IG page here: instagram.com/justbaebooks

Join our FB page here: facebook.com/authorjustbae

Best of regards,
Just Bae